A Painting for a Blind Man

And Other Stories

Valentine Williams

First Published in the UK in 2019 by Mantle Lane Press

Copyright © Valentine Williams 2019

The right of Valentine Williams to be identified as author of this work has been asserted by her.

This book is sold subject to the condition that it shall not, by the way of trade or otherwise, be lent, resold, hired out, or otherwise circulated without the publisher's prior consent in any form of binding or cover other than that in which it is published and without a similar condition, including this condition, being imposed on the subsequent purchaser.

ISBN 978-1-9998416-9-0

Mantle Lane Press
Springboard Centre
Mantle Lane
Coalville
LE67 3DW
www.mantlelanepress.co.uk
www.mantlearts.org.uk

Printed and bound in the UK by
Imprint Digital, Upton Pyne, Exeter, EX5 5HY

Cover illustration by Gabriella Marsh
gabriellamarsh.com

For P.J.W. with love and thanks.

Contents

A Painting for a Blind Man   7

"Come On In, The Water's Lovely"   22
And Other Lies

Daughters of the Revolution   33

Multi Storey   44

Quoth the Raven 'Nevermore'   55

A Painting for a Blind Man

Olivia wondered what it would be like to live in a world without light and colour. She dabbed a little ochre onto her palette and lifted the tip of her brush to sweep up the oily pigment and place it carefully on the still life on her easel. It was hard to imagine. She glanced across the lime-washed courtyard to the terrace. Brick-red geraniums, silver-dark olives, lipstick pink zinnias; the colours vibrated in the sunlight. Not being able to experience the vividness of those colours – what must that be like?

The visitors were discussing their plans for the day – should they walk down the valley to the river, or up into the hills? Or go to the beach instead? Olivia's husband Rob was offering advice.

"What do you think, Olivia?" he called across to her. "Is it better to walk up into the olive groves or down to the river? What do you think?"

Olivia, from the shade of her studio, considered the matter.

"Well, it'll get hot later. If you set off up the track through the olives, you'll be up there by late morning and you can have a picnic under the olives and stroll back downhill. Or wait until the sun dips a bit. You've got the lemon groves as well then."

"And downhill?"

"Well, it's a nice walk, but personally I'd go down in the late afternoon, have a beer in the taverna and come back when it's cooler. There's not much shade on that path." The guests considered their options. Rob went inside to wash up.

Rob and Olivia had been unsure how suitable a holiday it would be for Paul. There was a lot of rough ground and difficult walking, but they decided once they'd described what they were offering to leave it up to them.

Olivia could see Paul listening to her. His head tilted towards her and his nose was absorbing the scent of oregano, goat's dung and fig leaves. He tapped his stick to show he was paying attention.

"Up or down, Rosie?" His companion was weighing it up.

"Is it easy walking if we go up?" she asked Rob.

"Bit rough in places, but you should manage it."

Rosie held her stick in her right hand pointing backwards, and Paul took the end of it, following her as they set off up the rocky track.

Rob came in to see her when the visitors were safely on their way.

"Fancy a coffee?"

"Yes please. Will he cope on these tracks, do you think?"

"He seems quite determined. I'm sure they'll be fine."

Next morning after breakfast she heard Paul outside, working his way towards her with his stick.

"You're at the door now. There's a small step," she told him.

He stood just inside the door, dividing the light, his hand exploring the rough wall beside him.

A lizard was sucked into a hole near his foot. A smell came to him of oil-paint and turpentine and old damp rags. It was not a familiar smell to him, but he knew what it was. The turpentine smelled like the pine trees when the sun warmed them. Olivia saw the trees outside reflected in his dark glasses. He folded his stick and put it in his pocket. Olivia guessed he was curious. She waited.

"Hi, Paul."

"Painting already Olivia?"

"Yup. Get the best ideas early in the day."

"What do you paint?" It was an academic question, but he was curious.

"I paint what I see around me." He nodded. "I'm running out of ideas." An impulsive thought struck her: "I'd like to paint you something. But would there be any point?" Olivia stepped away from the easel and glanced over at Paul, wondering if she'd been insensitive or rude. But he was untroubled.

Paul tapped his feet on the floor. He was thinking. He took a while to answer and Olivia guessed he was trying to work out what had made her ask the question.

"Would there be any point?" he repeated.

"Yes. But the thing is, any painting I paint for you can be anything you want it to be. It's only limited by your imagination."

"Well - it's an intriguing thought."

"I could paint you a different picture for every day of your stay."

"In real paint? Oils? Watercolours? Or what? "

"I could use a mix. I could tell you about the painting – tell you its story – or you could tell me what you wanted me to paint. No, forget it, it's a mad idea." Paul was quiet, thinking.

"It's an interesting idea. Shall we give it a try?" He was excited now.

"I'll tell you what; have a think today about what you want me to paint and tell me after supper tonight. Yes - let's give it a try." She was intrigued by the idea too, even though it was mad.

At supper on the terrace the guests were going over the events of the day, and Rob was telling them about the history of the island. Paul was unusually quiet.

"Enjoy today, Paul?" asked Rosie. She was Paul's new wife and keen to make a good impression, as they hadn't been married long. They had swum and walked along the coastal path, while she learned how to steer him gently around prickly bushes and across potholes in the path, by going ahead of him with a stick and letting him take hold of it. He sometimes became impatient with her lack of useful commentary, but they had managed quite well despite this.

"Yes," he said, after some thought. "Rosie tells me she saw a snake, didn't you Rosie?"

"Yes. It wriggled off when we got near, but Paul heard it. Bit scary."

"What did it look like?" enquired Phil.

"Oh – brownish. You know." Olivia, at the other end of the table, listened carefully.

"Paul and I have an assignation after supper," she told them. "I'm going to paint Paul a picture. Maybe a snake could be in it?" The others looked slightly bemused. Paul was smiling.

"Yes, I know. Crazy idea," said Olivia. "But let's say it's an experiment."

Afterwards they sat together in the studio. Olivia had her sketch book on her knee and a fat, black pencil.

"What... um... are your impressions of today? What stands out for you?"

"Well, the snake was one. Oh, I don't know. Lots of things really..." his voice tailed off.

Olivia had a thought. "Imagine you've got a tray in your lap – that's the canvas if you like. Where would you like the snake to go?" He thought, and she could see his face working as he visualised it. His hands held an imaginary tray in front of him. Suddenly one hand moved in a sweep:

"The snake should be diagonally across, as if it's wriggling away." She drew the snake with exaggerated curves and took Paul's hand, guiding it along the snake's body.

"Here's its head." Their hands rested on the paper.

"Does it have a tongue?" he asked.

"I can give it one. Shall I put one in?" He nodded.

"Good. Now what colour is this snake? Describe it to me." As he was thinking she was adding to the sketch on the paper block on her lap. She went on, unsure because she didn't know him too well: "Do you remember colours? Forgive me asking."

"I'm not sure if what I think I remember are colours. I was very tiny when I lost my sight. When I dream, things aren't all the same. They're different colours. In my mind, the snake is a dull, metallic colour, sort of brown or bronze. I handled one once and I think it was actually quite brightly coloured, but what I felt was dark and shiny. No, paint this one a sort of brown, an interesting brown."

"There's a brown that is coppery, with a bit of pewter. A good snake colour. Is that...?"

"Sounds perfect. Are you painting it now?"

"Just sketching while we get our ideas together. And making notes. Tell me about where you both were when you saw it." Oops, she thought, he didn't see it. He was totally unconcerned by her question.

"We'd climbed up the headland. There were a lot of bushes and it was a bit rough going."

"Rough ground. Bushes." Deftly she drew them in. "Where was the sea? Left or right?"

"Left."

"And the sun?"

"Right. We had hats on, but the sun was pretty fierce."

"Anything else?"

"Insects. They made a lot of noise. There was a bird, too. Might have been a hawk. Rosie didn't know what it was."

"A hawk." With deft sweeps she drew the hawk, high at the top of the page. "Do you want you and Rosie in the picture?" He was silent for a moment.

"I don't think so," he said.

After he'd gone back to join Rosie, Olivia got her easel out and placed a blank canvas on it.

She sat and surveyed it for a long time. "What he's telling me to paint is his impression, his memory," she thought. "It's not what I see in front of me. And he can't see it anyway. What am I doing? I don't know how to make this picture tactile in any way. But maybe I don't have to. Maybe describing it in his own words to him and guiding his hand over it will be enough." She set to work.

The next day she showed it to him, taking his hand and tracing it around the things she'd painted.

"This is the rocky path." She moved his finger up and down along her brush marks. "There are prickly bushes here," she moved his hand to the side, "and they catch your clothes."

"And the insects are making a row. You've put in the insects?"

"Here they are." She moved his hand over the small blobs of paint. "And it's hot. The sun is bright, but over here" - she took his hand and moved it – "is the sea, all cool and delicious, with shade from the pine trees." He moved his hands slowly away from hers and allowed himself to feel the painting. She saw his face contort slightly. She touched his arm lightly, to reassure him.

Over the next few days, Olivia's paintings changed. She left behind perspective, scale and composition and focussed instead on the essential qualities of the objects; the prickliness of the bushes, the rockiness of the path, the snake's slither, the sun's heat. The effect was remarkable, but she wasn't satisfied.

Each day after supper, Paul came to her studio and they talked about the day. Shape and scent, taste and texture became important for her as he talked about eating local bread, olives and peaches. Olivia painted the things he described as if she couldn't see them, only experience them.

Swimming in the bay she painted as luscious circles, rippling out, pale feet touching smooth pebbles. She felt the water on her skin when she painted it, and shivered. She encouraged Paul to tell her about the smells, the sounds, and the sensations he experienced. Then she encouraged him to link this to how he was feeling at the time, drawing in other memories he had, other associations.

Every evening she told him about the painting she'd done the day before, tracing his hand over the surface and drawing the painting again in words for him, taking her time. Then they'd start on a new picture. He was fascinated by this process. Olivia tried to represent the sounds he'd heard – cicadas, wind in the pine trees, sand sliding down the shoreline, bazouki music – getting him to visualise and describe them. How do you paint the sound of wind in pine trees? She didn't know, but she did her best. They moved on to people he'd met.

"Takis. How would you describe him? What does he remind you of?"

"I think he's thin and quite old. Like a goat?"

"Colour? Shape?"

"The colour of the land. What colour is the earth around here?"

"Rich brown, with chunks of marble in it."

"Can you put that in? I think Takis is an irregular shape, like that, but his hands are important. He has a firm grip." Olivia sketched away. "He smells of tobacco."

The paintings were more abstract now. Olivia was amazed by them. Paul relived his experiences and Olivia was drawn in and began to realise that her relationship with Paul was deepening into something quite profound, and also that the next night would be their last.

Rosie was desperate to see the paintings and asked Olivia if she could send them back, but Olivia was cagey about this. She didn't want Rosie to see them, fearing she wouldn't understand what their work was about. Besides, there was something personal about them.

"I'll ask Paul which ones he wants to keep," she told

her. "He won't want them all." Secretly she was thinking that maybe she could pack up the ones he wanted for him to open when he got back to England.

Their next meeting was late, because they had eaten out on their last night and it was midnight before Olivia tucked Paul's hand under her elbow and led him to her studio.

"Don't keep him up too late," shouted Rosie after them. They were all a bit drunk.

The last painting she had done under his instruction was a painting of their courtyard, with Rob sitting reading under the red sunshade and Rosie sipping a drink. The olive tree and Olivia's chickens were in the background. There were lizards, and bougainvillea.

Olivia took his hand.

"Paul. Here's the tree we looked at, all bumps and lumps, yet the leaves are silky smooth. The chickens are strutting about on their strong yellow legs, eating melon rind and corn. Down here is Rosie, sipping her drink. Maybe she's a bit bored, as you said, and over here is Rob, reading his book. It's a warm evening and the night flowers are out, and the cicada is making a noise. You'll remember this night with this painting."

"You're not in the painting?"

"No. I have a special picture for you though, which is of me. I've put it into a tube, so you can take it with you." She paused. "Rosie wants to see what we've been doing. She asked me if you could take the paintings home. I said I'd ask you." His face showed his feelings:

"I have the pictures we did in my head. They're there forever. These are yours, to keep. After all, you painted them." She kissed him then. "Thank you, Olivia. This has meant a lot to me."

Rosie called them, and she led Paul out across the moonlit courtyard to their bedroom.

Rob was locking up and as she turned to go in he put an arm around her.

"Be sorry to see them go?" She nodded. "Yes, it's been good. The next ones arrive on Monday. Hey ho."

"He'll be sad to say goodbye to you." She smiled, a little sadly.

Paul held onto the sealed tube with the picture in it as he said his goodbyes. Rosie was eager to see what it contained and annoyed that Olivia hadn't let her see the paintings. It seemed that Paul was not going to take them home after all.

When Paul finally consented once they got home to opening the tube, inside was a sheet of textured handmade white paper with a message carefully dotted out in Braille on a label bearing the words 'This picture is of anything you want it to be. With love from Olivia.' Paul smiled, remembering.

"Come On In, The Water's Lovely" And Other Lies

"Come on in," called Chantelle. "The water's lovely."

It was a lie. The water was not lovely at all, but shockingly, chillingly, testicle-shrinkingly cold.

Edgar tried to accustom himself to it first by paddling, then splashing with his hands, until he knew with certainty that there was no way he was going to go in there, though the sun was still warm on the rocks and the air was mild. It was April and they were in Greece. She called him again, gaily, her red and white bikini glowing in the fading light, as she bobbed about, forty metres from where he stood on the shingle bank, protesting with every fibre of his being. He gave up and turned his back on her,

"Too cold. Sorry. I'll go in tomorrow when the sun's out." He strode up the beach, causing a small cascade of pebbles to slide down towards the quiet water.

"Coward!"

She tried to splash him, but he was well out of reach. She swam a few strokes towards him, then waded ashore and stood next to him, with tender pebble-dinted feet, and water streaming off her elbows and hair. He handed her the towel without speaking. Her lips were blue. She head-butted him playfully.

Dressed, they sat side by side on the crest of the shingle and watched the sea lick and lap the tide's edge. They were alone. He put his arm around her. She wriggled impatiently.

"You have cold hands."

"Not as cold as yours." He sighed and stood with difficulty, his knees creaking with the strain. She gave him the full double headlamp gaze from her big blue eyes and he melted.

"Oh Chantelle!"

"We should go back now."

She got up and brushed sand off his leg. Her French accent was charming. If only he could make her happy! He wished he was younger; nearer her age. But his age hadn't put her off at all, she said. She preferred older men.

He'd been alone too long, since Marion left. What was he? A father figure? If so, his feelings for Chantelle were decidedly incestuous. He thought she was waiting for him to make up his mind, and he couldn't, not really. It was a leap in the dark and he wasn't sure he could do it.

For Chantelle, this would be fourth time around. She'd been married twice and with a third partner for eight years and had taken numerous lovers, a fact she took no trouble to conceal. However, Edgar was flattered. She challenged him, made him feel alive. He tidied up when she was coming round and bought flowers to put on the table and wine he couldn't afford.

Back at their holiday apartment, Chantelle spread turquoise scarves over the plastic table on the balcony and lit a scented candle. He watched her warily.

"You are too tense. I shall relax you."

She began to knead his shoulders as he sat, poring over a crossword. She had changed into a white skirt and sequinned black top, which accentuated her small size, and she had wrapped a sky-blue silken scarf around her damp hair.

"Chantelle. You don't know what that does to me."

"Ha. I know very well. You are a naughty man."

"I'm a very lucky one."

"Yes, you are, Edgar. We two, we are both lucky I think."

It was the second evening of their holiday and the first time they had been away together. Her daughter was with her father. He thought his adult children knew about Chantelle, but he wasn't certain.

Chantelle's daughter knew about him. He'd once taken her on a school trip, and Chantelle had been waiting for the coach when they returned. She was still with Armand then. He'd thought then how attractive she was and was mesmerised by her blue eyes and smile when she thanked him for looking after her daughter.

Edgar sat on the balcony and watched the world go by while Chantelle draped her silken scarves over the furniture and lit the candles.

"When do we meet the others?"

She stopped what she was doing. "'Half past eight. You have to get changed."

"Shall I wear the blue shirt?"

"As you wish." She shrugged expressively. He got to his feet and went inside to search through the clothes Chantelle had stored in the wardrobe. He looked himself over in the mirror. No, he wouldn't wear the blue shirt; it was too thin and made his arms look skinny. He still had some hair, at any rate, and he was as slim as he'd been in his youth. He put on a dark top, brushed his hair and clipped some long hairs that were spiking out of his eyebrows. Why did hair do that when you got older? There was a knock at their door. He opened it cautiously. It was Sally from the next apartment.

"Coming?" Sally's eyes registered the candles and cloths. Edgar answered "We're ready. Chantelle?"

"I am coming." She appeared at his side and they set off, with Sally's husband Andrew in the lead.

Edgar tried to find something in common with Andrew as they walked. The path was uneven, needing repair after the spring rains and they walked slowly. By common agreement they settled on music. Both were jazz lovers, and Edgar was looking forward to an interesting conversation. Chantelle slipped her arm through Edgar's when the path widened and gave Andrew the full beam of her blue eyes.

"I have to go with him to this music. I do not understand jazz; you have to explain it to me."

Chantelle, there's nothing to explain. You don't like it, that's all."

But Andrew was keen to help: "Did you mean that you wish you understood why it's different from other music? What makes jazz, jazz?" She was nodding emphatically. She turned on Edgar with a little pout.

"Edgar, you never try to explain."

"It's not that easy to explain. Like abstract art." Still she gazed at him accusingly.

"Let me try," Andrew offered. They strolled on down the hill to the restaurant with Edgar now forced to turn his attention to Sally, who also didn't understand jazz and didn't want to talk.

The conversation was hard work and he was uncomfortably aware of Chantelle just ahead of him gazing at Andrew's face as he expounded on improvisation and why Thelonius Monk was so great.

"He lived in France!" Chantelle declared with glee. Andrew was captivated.

"So he did. You think that's what made him great?"

"Of course!"

Edgar butted in,

"He only lived in France at the end of his life. He was a sick man."

"But still…" She turned her gaze back to Andrew, who was waiting to tell her about jazz musicians he had heard play in Paris. Sally appeared not to mind but Edgar felt sidelined. A third couple joined them in the restaurant, people they'd met on the plane, and the evening rolled along.

All through the meal Chantelle held court, turning the spotlight of her eyes on each of the three men in turn. Sally and Brenda, the other woman, discussed their children and work, through mouthfuls of fried aubergine and tomato salad.

Sally held her glass up. "Cheers, everyone." Andrew reluctantly turned his attention away from Chantelle.

"Cheers!" They clinked glasses.

"Do you understand about jazz now?" enquired Sally, mischievously.

"Yes but I will forget. You, you will have to tell me

again, Edgar." There was a slight pettishness in her voice. He gazed at her like an indulgent uncle addressing a child.

"I'll tell you anything, any time, Chantelle."

"I don't think so. Andrew will have to remind me."

"Chantelle likes to keep people busy. Don't you, Chantelle?" Edgar did not expect an answer. Sally tried to divert them:

"Anyone decided yet which beach is the best?" Edgar spoke up.

"Chantelle and I tried out the one you can see from the road. The water was freezing. Chantelle went in but I didn't."

"I should think it's a bit cold yet," commented Sally.

"Edgar, you are always afraid."

"You will learn Chantelle, that one of the benefits of being older is that you can choose not to do things you don't want to do. I chose not to go in. Simple as that."

She pouted and rearranged her scarf.

"But I wanted you with me!" Flattered, he took another mouthful of wine and surveyed her.

"She wanted me with her! What do you do with this woman?"

She snuggled up to him and he put his arm around her. She looked small and pretty and Sally suddenly felt like a carthorse next to a palomino colt. Brenda was gazing at the sea; Andrew was searching for more wine. Brenda's partner Geoff was gazing at Chantelle as though he'd like to eat her.

Back in their apartment that night, Chantelle appeared quiet and withdrawn.

"Tired darling? What's the matter?"

"Nothing. I have a headache."

"Can I find you a paracetamol?" She nodded. He fetched one and sat next to her, not knowing what to do or say.

"We're a right pair, aren't we?" he said finally. "We see each other all week, but we don't live together. We come on holiday together, we get along fine, but we're not committed in the way the others are. And that suits me, I suppose."

She said nothing, just sat with one hand on her forehead.

"Let's not spoil what we have, Chantelle. Let's leave it the way it is."

"And how is that?"

"Lovers. People who like one another. A lot." He kissed her on the cheek.

"I do not have good luck with lovers."

"Well, you haven't had good luck with husbands either. Neither have I."

"Silly! I've only had two husbands."

"Only two?"

"Now you are teasing me."

"I thought you wanted us to get married Chantelle?"

"No, I never wanted this. You think because I am nice to your friends that I will make you jealous? You will want to be married to me to keep me for yourself perhaps? I do not want this, Edgar. I am a free woman."

"So you don't want me to ask you to marry me?"

"Poof! What difference does it make?"

Edgar liked the fact that other men envied him and found her attractive and it was partly what kept him at her side. Yet he was in a state of constant anxiety about losing her. He thought about that. She slept with him, she was there for him when he needed a female companion; she lit up the place with her scarves and candles and scented oils. He knew he'd never be bored with her around. But there was still the fear; the fear that she would find someone else irresistibly attractive and want to go off with them. She'd done it before. He answered at last.

"It would be a commitment. Your mother might like it. Your daughter might, as well. We don't have to live together…"

"What is the point? I like a certain freedom…" He felt he'd failed a test, but he didn't know what the test might be. She got ready for bed. She wasn't looking at him.

"Per'aps we go to the beach again tomorrow?" Her pink feet slid down into the bed. "Maybe you will go in the water this time?"

But he knew he wouldn't.

Daughters of the Revolution

The Daughter crept up from her bedroom in the basement holding her head and treading delicately.

"I feel ill," she moaned. Jenni, her mother, and almost-aunt Naomi were making tea in the ground floor flat. They glanced at her, cautiously.

"Don't be sympathetic or anything." She paused to see what the effect was.

"Poor baby," said her mother unsympathetically.

"I don't need the sarcasm. All right?" said The Daughter, as if every word hurt her. "Have you got an aspirin? Or something?"

"Drink lots of water," said her mother briskly. "I'll find you an aspirin in a minute. You're old enough to know not to drink so much. I mean. Bloody hell."

Naomi wasn't sure whether to be sympathetic or to ignore her. The Daughter's eyes narrowed with pain. She steered herself towards the sofa and tossed the top layer of cushions onto Naomi's recently vacated fold-up bed. Underneath was cloth from friends in Angola, rugs from Chile, blankets from Peru; cushions and quilts from all corners of the globe. All Jenni's memories were caught up in these gifts. Most of it was too moth-eaten and cat-mauled to keep but too pretty or interesting to throw away. Each told its own story, and in every one Jenni had played a part.

As The Daughter, Celeste, made a nest for herself, the two cats leapt off the Peruvian end of the sofa hastily, giving her a dirty look. She sank down, snatched back a blanket, and covered her eyes with the back of her hand.

The two women sat in silence at the table with their tea.

"I think I'm going to throw up," announced Celeste, rising unsteadily to her feet and moving like a sleepwalker towards the toilet under the stairs.

"Well, go," urged her mother, not looking at her.

The cats mewed for their food, or to be let out, Naomi wasn't sure which, but to help her friend she offered to see to them. They followed her to the garden door, but it was triple locked, and Naomi couldn't find the keys. Blocking the garden door were piles of Searchlight magazines, Solidarity posters, old anoraks, empty plant pots, bags of cat litter and dog leads. She returned to Jenni who was standing distractedly by the window, her hair crazily disturbed around her shoulders, trying not to worry about The Daughter. The cats followed her.

The dog came in from the hall and sat at her feet, looking beseechingly at her with his collie's eyes. He raised a paw hoping she'd notice and take him for a walk.

Jenni wasn't ready for a walk. She got tired easily and was often upset about small things.

"Down, Boy! Down!" she told him, and he slunk under the table with sad, accusing eyes. Slightly guilty, Jenni picked up a squeaky rubber ball and .tossed it to the far end of the room, where Celeste, who had returned from the lavatory to the sofa island, lay with her eyes closed and a martyred look on her face. Boy dashed after the ball with piercing squeaks, yaps and growls. Celeste was outraged.

"Jenni! I know it's my fault I've got a hangover, but please..." she whined indignantly.

"Can I walk Boy for you?" offered Naomi, trying to be helpful. She noted the fact that in the year since she had last seen her, Celeste was calling her mother by her first name. Were they now equals? The Daughter was nineteen, but small and afraid of many things: sleeping alone with the light off, loud noises, brothers.

Naomi found the dog's lead on the empty plant stand by the door, and summoned Boy.

"Walkies!"

Jenni was dressed when she returned, but seemed distracted. She wore her glasses all the time and looked strangely naked without them. It was early days, Naomi reflected. She'd had a lot to cope with.

Celeste lay, silently now, on the sofa with her eyes closed, her black hair fluffed out against an orange-and-brown-striped pillow. Her nose stud sparkled in the light from the window.

Naomi's bed had all the things piled on it that had been on the sofa, including a cat who wasn't sure she was meant to be there, the Saturday edition of The

Guardian, and all of her own bedding that she hadn't yet tidied. Naomi looked past Celeste into the back garden, and saw a cherry tree in full bloom and a garden chair.

"Garden looks nice, Jenni."

"I paid an awful man to come and clear it. Ghastly. I can't tell you."

"He did a good job though, looking at it. Why was he so awful?"

"Jenni, do you have to discuss it now?" Celeste complained.

The two women moved away from the window, drank coffee quietly at the table and read The Guardian. Naomi, interested in Jenni's observations, checked out the news: Israel, Hamas, Cuba, Venezuela, Bolivia, Mugabe.

"I helped fund Zanu-PF before Mugabe came to power. Remember? We went to a meeting in Mayor Street when you lived in Dalston." Jenni remembered.

"I mean, land reforms were necessary, but Mugabe's gone about it in the wrong way…" And so they discussed matters.

Largely their views coincided, as they had when

they were young women, fighting the National Front, attending protest rallies and supporting the Sisterhood. Then Naomi had opted for a quieter life and Jenni had stayed in London. She was involved in so many different causes and had so many contacts that Naomi found it hard to keep up.

Now Jenni the revolutionary, a woman of soft edges and heart and steely courage, was collapsing inwardly like one of those balloons that shrink over time to a shrivelled puff of skin containing stale air.

The fight had gone out of her.

Celeste perked up in the afternoon, while Naomi and Jenni were out shopping, and was sitting up drinking tea and watching Desperate Housewives when they returned.

"Feeling a bit better?" enquired Naomi fondly.

"A bit," she conceded, playing with her earring. "I know I shouldn't have done it."

"What were you drinking?"

"Oh all sorts. I wasn't thinking. They had a domestic at the end of the evening, so I came home."

"How awful."

"Who had a domestic?" queried Jenni, alerted to danger in her daughter's life.

"The girl whose birthday it was. They were both drunk. I came home with the boys."

"Doesn't sound like a great evening," commented Naomi.

"It wasn't," replied Celeste truthfully.

"People tend to row more when they're drunk," said Naomi, unnecessarily. "It's not good to be around it, though. Who won?"

"Oh nobody won," said Celeste, irritably. "Anyway, I left. I told you."

"Oh yes. Sorry."

Naomi took her friend out for a meal in the evening. Celeste wasn't up to eating much and opted to stay in with some hummus and olives. The restaurant was supposed to be serving soul food, and they did see curry goat and rice and peas on the menu, but the cook was Turkish and the meal was neither Turkish nor Jamaican. While they were together, they talked of their children. It was easier when none of them were listening.

"How's Charles?" enquired Naomi. "Still sticking it out at his job?"

Jenni told her she worried about her eldest son's new partner, a beautiful but calculating Libyan girl who wasn't supposed to be in the country. Jenni felt her son was being used.

"He's a bit naïve like that," she concluded.

"You think he's making a mistake?"

"I don't know. He's besotted with her." This time Charles had kept his girlfriend away from his mother, aware of her misgivings. Jenni seemed resigned. It was clear she missed him. "It's his life," she said, not meaning it.

"And hers," added Naomi. Then, "And you've got your life, too, now."

Jenni nodded. It was taking a while to sink in. To let go, to be without them - it was hard, Naomi could see that. She'd only just managed it herself.

Naomi thought she ought to help clear up the kitchen when they got home. Celeste had gone out.

On the kitchen shelf above the dish-filled sink was a Rude Girl mug, cartons of green tea, coffee in jars and packets, brown sugar, various cups and bowls and a hand drawn sign saying: 'DO NOT SOD UP THE ARRANGEMENTS.'

Naomi washed up and tried to put things away. There was no spare surface anywhere. Jenni, grateful and resentful, watched as her friend searched for spaces to store things in.

"If I wasn't so tired…" Jenni said.

"You've had a lot to cope with. You're still coping with a lot."

"I just have to get on with my life."

"Way to go, girl. You have to look after you and enjoy your life, now you've found Phil. When are you seeing him again?"

"Next weekend. No, it's good. It's all good."

"I'll have to meet him. Bring him down one weekend."

The revolutionary posters in the hall were curled at the edges. Soon they would be taken down. The house would be sold. Jenni would either join her new partner or drift on here in a new flat. It wouldn't be the same. What would she do with all her books; all those papers?

A discussion with Celeste about her degree took up some of the next morning. Impressively, she was in line for a First. She was reading complex tomes about world banking, money movement and private finance initiatives. Naomi couldn't begin to follow it. Celeste lost interest in the conversation and got her books out, after a row with her mother about space to do homework on the table.

Jenni promised to move her piles of papers, sighing deeply as she did so. Slightly mollified, Celeste settled down to work.

Celeste had plans to live with her boyfriend in Venezuela after her graduation. Jenni had no plans to stand in her way. Her brother, Mark, upstairs with his new partner, had thrown his mother's things out as he emptied the rooms that had once been hers. He had done this with anger and regret, mixed with a measure of love. He brought things down in batches: shoes, paper shredder, books, folders, pictures. He left them by the front door. He had filled one skip already. His girlfriend Shyra was a member of the Communist Party and he thought he ought to join too, in homage to his parents. Jenni was less enthusiastic about it than he had hoped.

The stuff from the upstairs rooms formed a wall that effectively divided the house. Jenni would not go up unless invited. Shyra was up there, cleaning and decorating and organising Jenni's son and their belongings. They had their own door. Things were changing.

Naomi met Mark on the stairs as she was leaving to catch her train the next day.

"Next time I come you'll have to show me what you've done up there. If Shyra doesn't mind."

"Yeah. There have been a lot of changes. Glad you could come. Mum needs her friends." Naomi, who'd known him as a baby, saw that he was now a tall, friendly, handsome young man with nice manners. He'd be nearly thirty now, and something in him had grown up since she'd last seen him, in the year his father died.

"Say goodbye to your brothers for me?"

"No problem. Bye." He leaned over and kissed her cheek. "Take care."

She loved him; she loved all of them, including the dead and missing ones, but the counter-revolution was underway.

Multi-Storey

Multi-storey car parks filled him with horror, even on a good day, and this was not a good day.

Too often he'd found they were empty, dirty, soulless spaces, smelling of piss and abandoned dreams.

The entrance to the car park on Dunlin Street was unusual. It just didn't look right. He sat in the car for a moment contemplating it. Drive in, go up the ramps, find a space, park, come down in the lift or on the stairs. Of course, it was simple. What was he getting stressed about? He took the ticket from the machine with reluctance and watched the barrier lift like a broken arm to let him through.

The clockwise spiral, even though he drove up

it slowly and carefully, made him feel a little dizzy. There was an exit on each bend, but it didn't look as though there were many spaces. A thought crossed his mind. How did one get out? He'd work that out later. Near the top of the ramp he found a space. Slowly he pulled over, left the spiral ramp and parked next to an old Saab. The columns dividing up the spaces had been scraped where car owners had parked badly. He noticed things like that. He'd left enough room to open the door and get out, with some room to spare. Not like some other idiots. He found his gloves in the side-pocket, straightened his tie, grabbed his folder from the passenger seat and got out of the car.

He'd done it. The sign on the wall showed an arrow to the lift, and a notice saying 'Exit'.

He was glad he'd managed it and not had to park further away in the famous Seventies car park over the bus station that he hated so much. It was a listed building now – a listed building!

He despaired sometimes. What merit could it possibly have? He'd used it before, out of necessity, but mostly what he remembered about it was the duffle-coated toothless beggar loitering like a graveside companion by the coffee dispenser. Which didn't work anyway.

He had tried to leave the bus station via one of the subways then. There was no other way out.

He wasn't going to walk across the bus apron and get knocked over, and he could still feel the fear of stepping into this dimly lit tunnel, though as far as he could recall it had been empty. What he dreaded in subways was to see a figure appear at the far end and stand there, brandishing a knife. His dreams were full of scenes like these. He couldn't watch A Clockwork Orange without shuddering.

This time he'd been advised to use the corkscrew ramp arrangement in the multi-storey on Dunlin Street and he'd parked. On what level? He realised he wasn't sure. But he'd find it.

The lift took him to street level, and he hurried to his meeting at the Magistrates' Court.

His court appearance went badly and he felt as though he'd been slapped. The fine – it was for something really trivial for goodness sake – was out of all proportion to the crime. He had difficulty even thinking of it as a crime. What had he done? Used red diesel and been found out. Well, what did people do who had no money for fuel and had to be somewhere? Especially when there was plenty of the stuff knocking around in the tractor shed up at Ed's. There were days when he felt that everything he did was likely to be criticised one way or another.

Thinking about it made him angry, and he whacked his clip-file on the wall on his way out of the court. Yes, he was angry. He hadn't had any lunch and it was likely he'd lose a day's pay, having to drive here and back. Still, he might get back in time to escape the attention of his boss, who thought he was at the doctor's. Another lie that could be found out, he realised.

He passed office workers; shoppers heading for the car park and the bus station. He entered the car park through the back door where the lift was and pressed the button. The doors opened, revealing a large pale woman with a pushchair and a grubby toddler, who made room for him.

"Which floor?" he asked her, trying to be helpful..

"Six. Thanks." She smiled at him. He pressed six. Then he realised he'd forgotten his own landing number. It was quite high up. Maybe it was six too. The lift began its upward journey, stopping at four to open the doors to an elderly man with a walking stick who thought he was going down, but was quite unperturbed to be going up first.

"I quite like lifts," he told them. "Course, we should use the stairs really."

Stairs? It hadn't occurred to him that there might be stairs. But he'd come down in the lift and now he was going up in one. On level six the pale woman hauled the child and buggy out of the lift, and he wondered whether to follow her. He couldn't see his car. Maybe he'd go on up to the next level just to check.

On Level 7 there was a gap where he thought his car had been. His tired eyes took in the marks on the bay dividers, the pools of oil on the grey concrete floor. There was another car there, a hatchback. Had his car been stolen? He must have been mistaken, he thought, and got back in the lift, this time opting to go right to the top. Surely he hadn't driven right to the top to park? Had he? Level 8 seemed to be the top level. He felt exposed. He wouldn't like to be wandering round here at night, he thought, noticing a woman's shoe discarded by the wall. It was badly lit, badly signposted too.

He got out on Level 8, hearing the lift doors close behind him, and looked at where his car should be. Nothing. It couldn't have been this floor, he thought, logically, and took the lift down again, stopping this time on the seventh floor. Of course his car was not there. He felt as if some evil dream had enveloped him. He was beyond wanting to swear and kick things. Numbed and resigned, he was turning to go back down when he noticed a door further along the bay. He approached it, curiously. Why had he not noticed it before?

With an effort he pushed it open. He appeared to be in an offshoot of an old shopping mall. Grey walls twisted along a wide corridor, broken up by shop windows, which when he looked, were the interior walls of cafes and cinemas. He smelled popcorn and pizzas, could see people quite close to the window gazing at one another or stuffing wedges of pizza into their mouths. Nothing had prepared him for this. He knocked on the window and the diners looked up, startled. He gestured to them. Where was the entrance? He wanted to come in, he told them, making eloquent gestures that ended with him holding up both hands and mouthing "How do I get in?" The diners looked startled, but instead of responding in a way that was helpful, one youth made an 'I don't know' gesture, which was infuriating, and then they completely ignored him.

He shouted, "Hello? Hello?" They continued to ignore him. The corridor had a door at the end with a fire escape. He couldn't open it. He walked back past the glass windows that shielded the diners, who were now, it seemed to him, drinking large amounts of wine.

"Pull yourself together," he told himself. "Use your common sense." This was what his mother would have said, exasperated with him. He leant on the wall where his car should have been.

Again the question came: had it been stolen? He took the lift up again and walked down, feeling danger on the ramps as cars came up towards him and he had to duck into the bays. What should he do? He became more certain his car had been stolen. When he reached ground level he paused, found his mobile, and called the police station. He gave a description to the police, who were courteous and logged everything he told them. What should he do now? A car passed him, heading away from the multi story. Where had it come from? He walked round the central core of the building and found the anticlockwise spiral of the exit ramp. Presumably the car had come from there. It looked exactly like the ramp he'd driven up when he arrived.

He felt disorientated and strange. Where was the crossover point? He hadn't noticed it at the top of the first ramp, but it must be there. Or maybe there was one on each level and he'd somehow missed it.

He gave up and went off to find a cafe and some lunch. His diary and work papers were in the car. Without them he felt impotent. He phoned work and told them his car had been stolen. His boss sounded disbelieving and impatient with him, but at least he'd covered himself.

"Yes, of course the Police have been informed. Sorry? I said I'll try to make up the time tomorrow. Right now I'm just concerned to get the car back. No, I appreciate it's not an ideal situation. I'm really sorry." He ended the call.

His phone rang unexpectedly, vibrating in his pocket in a most unnerving way.

The police were going to pay him a visit. When would he be available?

"Because my bloody car's been stolen, I'm in a cafe on Town Hall Street wondering what the heck to do. I'm not going anywhere. Half an hour? Okay, I'll wait."

Half an hour later he looked at his watch. Then he pushed away the coffee cups in front of him on the dirty table and stood up. It was raining outside. Damn! His coat was in the car.

He spotted the police car further down the street. Well, at least they kept their promise, he thought, scurrying along the pavement to meet them. The copper in the driving seat looked him up and down as he approached, before lowering his window:

"Mr Smailes? I understand your car has been stolen?"

"That's correct."

"When did you leave your car? I've got the registration number as..." he looked at his notes.

"I've already given you all the details. At 10.15 this morning I arrived, parked the car, came down in the lift, and went to my meeting. I returned at 12.30 and it had gone. Since then I've been up and down every floor, and it's not here. It's been stolen. There's no other explanation."

"Do you want to get into the car Sir? You can show me where you think it should be."

"You think I'm making it up? That it hasn't been stolen at all?" Suddenly he felt frightened.

"Not at all, Sir. But we need to check before we log it as a theft. Now, shall we drive up?" He got in. A smell of damp clothes and stale tobacco filled the car. He wasn't sure if it was his smell, or if it was already there. The police officer took his time checking in with the station. It allowed him to calm down a little.

They approached the barrier. The arm went up and they drove slowly up the ramp, going clockwise.

There was his car, right on the bend of the sixth – or was it seventh? – landing.

"That's it! Stop the car!" How had he not realised it would be on the parallel ramp?

The policeman didn't comment, but stopped the car and allowed him to get out, parking the police car a few spaces further on. He folded his arms, resting his head on the roof of his car. He banged his head on the roof in a gesture of absolute despair.

The policeman came up behind him, quietly.

"You're quite certain this is your car, Sir? Can you give me the registration number again?"

But for the life of him he couldn't.

Quoth the Raven 'Nevermore'

Mercedes, the elegant and beautiful one, who stands apart from all others, watches from the window of her expensive Mayfair apartment, and muses:

Blowing hot and cold is something I'm good at. I like to faire la betise, it excites me, and it keeps them interested, especially Eddie. What a sucker. He has little boy eyes and a silly grin. I could slap him; really I could slap him hard; he deserves it for being so stupid. Muy stupido. Slapping is not what he wants; it's too real. He requires ritual. These boys have no idea how to handle a woman like me. They run around after me begging me to let them help me, begging for crumbs from my table and disappointed if I give them to them.
"Oh Miss Mersha," they say, "let me do that for you." Saps! I despise them. Clean my shoes or whatever. They jump to attention. I could punish them by refusing to let them do

things for me, but why should I? You reward a masochist by refusing to give him the punishment he craves. Good huh? I thought so once, but I'm getting bored. When I get bored, watch out, because then I'm nice, so nice you don't want to know me. I run my nails along Eddie's thigh when he takes me to the expensive restaurant where I like to eat and he looks like a stupid dog I've just patted. He tried to place his hand on my knee the other night, and I had a rage right there in the restaurant and told him never to presume such a thing again. He apologized at once. Muy stupido. He has begun to stammer a little when he speaks to me. I like it. It shows he is nervous.

Of course, he hopes he will sleep with me, they all do. So I torment them a little, allow them to hope for heaven, but it never comes. They prefer punishment from me, I think.

I keep the instruments in the big cupboard, with the special mirror. Eddie likes to be locked inside while I deal with Antoine. He almost suffocates, but when I relent and let him out, he is so grateful. Antoine dare not object to Eddie being present. He likes him to be there, and to come out of the cupboard when I pull the lead, and when Eddie shows he is excited Antoine likes to watch me punish him. You will think I am heartless, but I am born to please. Again and again they visit me, these two, and again and again I keep them guessing and waiting. I have expensive tastes and Papa always said I should have the best. It has been almost a year since… but I push the thoughts away.

Eddie comes from a wealthy family and has money to spare. He is well known as a barrister and spends his time when he is not with me racing cars. This is so boring for me, so Antoine amuses me on these occasions.

Antoine is not rich, but he has class. He was sent away to a seminary when he was young, he tells me, and he was beaten regularly. He deserved it he says, and maybe even he misses it. This makes it easy for him to come to me and enjoy the punishment I give. He likes my shoes with spike heels. I walk all over him and he never says a word.

Back home, such things are understood. It is a simple thing, this need for punishment. How lucky that they found me to give it to them. Ha - you think I am a whore, puttana, a cul, but I take no money from them. They buy me presents, of course they do, but Papa provided well for me and I do not need their money. No, I do this for love, and for the sense of power that it gives me. Eddie would like to have my power, but he cannot. His power is in knowing he can refuse to obey me - if he wishes - and neither of us will be satisfied. So who is the winner then?

Mersha pauses in her thoughts. Eddie comes to the door. He strokes his bald head with one hand and straightens his collar with the other while he stands on the step, waiting for the door to be opened. Sometimes it is a long wait. If he looks untidy he will be punished. He wants to be punished, but the game is not to invite punishment, but to court it slowly. He tries his best to please her. Miss Mersha (he prefers her real name, Mercedes) eventually presses the remote access button, which allows him to enter her apartment. Already he feels excited and knows he will have to work hard to conquer it before she accuses him of unacceptable behaviour. But today Mersha comes towards him and allows him to approach her and to inhale her perfume before he is dismissed to await her in the drawing room. He sits, wondering whether to read the magazine she has left out on the table. His shoes feel tight and uncomfortable; he has been in court most of the day and his feet are tired, while his wig has left an uncomfortable mark on his bald scalp. His nails are beautifully manicured and his shirt cuffs pristine. He dares not arrive in any other fashion. Mersha sometimes accompanies him to lunches with fellow barristers and he remembers that they dug each other in the ribs in the gentlemen's lavatory and congratulated him.

"Lucky dog."

"Don't know what he's done to deserve such a fine filly."

"Damn good pair of legs, what?"

Mersha, beautiful in a cream linen suit, enters the room, her large sensuous mouth lipsticked in slick red. Her black hair swings in precise angles around her neck. She smiles at him ominously. He feels his knees collapse, his belly fold into water. How desperately he desires her!

He bows his head and looks at his nails. Silence.

Should we feel sorry for Eddie, seeking his own punishment? He needs it; he has been a bad person and seeks restitution through suffering; only by being punished will he forgive himself. At length Mersha speaks:

"I see you have brought me no flowers."

"No, Miss Mersha."

"You know what this means?"

He shakes his head, slowly. He knows what it means; eventually it means punishment. He had not intended this; he had genuinely forgotten her flowers (orchids) in his excitement to get to her apartment on time.

"What else can you do for me?" She stands over him, dominating his world, her slim legs shimmering in their silky stockings, a tiny corner of expensive lace visible in the open neck of her shirt. He likes the details, he likes thinking about them; details are part of his life, a trace of lipstick, hair on a coat collar, a scratch where a fingernail gauged a chunk of flesh from an invading hand. Mersha is a perfectionist, a stickler, as his mother would say. He will never please her; that is all part of the arrangement.

"I came to invite you to the Opera." Mersha is taken aback. This is quite unexpected.

"What makes you think I would go to the Opera with you?" she asks, as if the idea is preposterous.

"It's Glyndebourne, tomorrow afternoon, and it's a production of 'The Tales of Hoffman'. A bit hackneyed I know, but some pretty tunes. It's my birthday. I did hope you would come."

The words tumble out. Now he can see how impossible it is. Of course she would not want to come. How could he imagine a woman like her would tolerate his company for a whole afternoon? He sighs. It will be his birthday tomorrow, his fiftieth birthday. He had hoped she would agree, yet realizes he knew she would not.

"I will come," says Madame the dominatrix, unexpectedly, "if you pay the price."

"What is the price? What do you want me to do?"

"Do not look at me when I am speaking to you. Keep your head down and your eyes on the floor.

This is the game. He knows it, understands it. He will have to suffer for her company. But that is what he came here for. Isn't it? The game will continue along the prescribed pattern. She will inflict some task on him, one he will fail at. Then he will be chastised. Antoine is not here, so this will be a solitary punishment, in the private room with the blood red walls and the black leather upholstery. She will select from her collection of implements one which matches her mood, and she will stop just short of actual physical harm, although this boundary has become more and more difficult to identify of late. They will not touch sexually. Remote access is in every way the essence of their union. He waits, head bowed.

Mersha walks slowly across the Aubusson carpet and gazes out of the window, one slim hand extending to the air, long polished finger-nails describing circles like questing antennae, her face unreadable. The soft autumn sunshine warms the few crab-apples left behind on the tree and the golden light reflects on her olive skin. Mersha is lost in a dream:

It was a day like this when... but I am Mersha, icy and hard, yielding just enough to allow hope to surface, then brutally stamping on it. Why have I forgotten the plot suddenly? Papa – yes, Papa is dead. Papa. It doesn't matter, it's not important, but it stops my mind from working. Eddie is puzzled. Why have I stopped, what was the price he had to pay for boring me to death with his company? But I have lost interest.

Eddie feels trouble in the air. Antoine, whom he

has got to know, is more able to respond appropriately. Eddie wishes Antoine were here, to share this strange dangerous calm.

The room feels hot. Mersha is staring out of the window. He coughs, quietly, to gain her attention, expecting to be chastised. Mersha turns to him slowly, her eyes like dark plums. Something has happened; her face is different. Eddie waits to see what will happen, holding his breath, not moving a muscle. A tear, a large slow tear like a drop of glass grows fat and hangs from her bottom eyelid, rolls down and disperses on her cheek. *This is not fair,* thinks Eddie, *this is not in my script at all. What the hell do I do now?* He stays perfectly still, waiting to see what will happen next.

And nothing happens, except that Mersha continues to stand there, tears rolling down her face one by one, silently. She is not with Eddie at all. After a while he stands up slowly and makes his way to the door, closing it quietly but firmly behind him.

No more, nevermore, he thinks. *Quoth the raven, 'Nevermore'.* In the street a car stereo is playing *'Say Goodbye to Love.'*

He feels curiously empty. It will pass. He will be fifty tomorrow, time to grow up. He will take his clerk to the Opera instead.

Mersha stands, hearing the door click shut as Eddie leaves. For the first time since her father's death she cries, long, choking sobs. She will spend the evening alone, and Eddie will not return. She knows this; he knows this. It's over.

When ice melts, water forms, tears flow, rivers run. Who can say when that time is in the human heart? Sometimes it never comes, the pack ice covers the deep waters of the spirit. Only a fool would venture in.

Desire is hot, it flows like molten metal, it is orange, fiery, dangerous, alive. Tears have extinguished it.

Acknowledgements

This publication was supported using public funding by the National Lottery through Arts Council England

Mantle Lane Press would like to acknowledge support from Writing West Midlands.

Mantle Lane Press is a subsidiary of Mantle Arts Limited, which receives financial support from North West Leicestershire District Council.